# THE PRINCE AND THE PAUPER

# THE PRINCE AND THE PAUPER

by
## Mark Twain

Adapted by
Nicole Vittiglio

Illustrated by
Dave Hopkins

Modern Publishing
A Division of Unisystems, Inc.
New York, New York 10022

Series UPC: 38150

Cover art by Marcel Laverdet

# Contents

# CHAPTER 1

# Born Into Poverty

On an autumn day in London in the second quarter of the sixteenth century, a boy was born to a poor family named Canty. The new baby, called Tom, was not a welcome addition. He was wrapped in rags.

On the same day, another boy was born to a rich family by the name of Tudor. He was called Edward Tudor, Prince of Wales, and he was a very welcome addition. All of England had been awaiting his birth. Feasts and parades were held in his honor. He was wrapped in satin and silk.

The streets of London were very narrow, crooked and dirty—especially in the part of town where Tom lived, not far from London Bridge. His rickety house stood on a foul street called Offal Court. Other families shared the cramped house with the Cantys.

Tom's mother and father had an old bed, which stood in the corner of their small one-room apartment. Tom, his grandmother, and his two sisters, Nan and Bet, slept on the floor.

Bet and Nan were twins. They were good-hearted girls, but dirty and clothed in rags. They were not very smart, but they were kind, like their mother. Tom's father and the grandmother were nasty people. John Canty was a thief, and his mother was a beggar. They made beggars of the children, but failed to make the children thieves.

A priest named Father Andrew lived in an apartment in the same house. He was a good man. Secretly, he taught the children right from wrong. He also taught Tom a little Latin, and how to read and write.

All of the houses in Offal Court were similar to the Canty house. Riots and brawls were common, as was hunger. Little Tom had a hard life, but he did not know it. It was the sort of life that all the boys that lived in Offal Court had. Tom thought that it was the only kind of life to have.

When Tom came home empty-handed at night, after a day of unsuccessful begging, his father would curse him and hit

him. Then his grandmother would take over. In the middle of the night, his starving mother would slip him any measly scrap of food she had managed to save. If her husband caught her, he would beat her, too.

Often, Tom would get through such nights by thinking about the wonderful castles, kings, and princes that Father Andrew had told him about. Tom dreamed so much about royalty that he began to hate his life in Offal Court. Soon, Tom began to act and speak like a prince. His behavior was so convincing that adults began to ask for his advice.

After a while, Tom organized a royal court among his friends. He was the prince and his friends were his court. After a day of pretending, Tom would beg for a few pennies and go home to his miserable scraps. But his desire to become a prince grew all the time. It became the passion of his life.

# CHAPTER 2

# Tom Meets a Real Prince

One day, Tom woke up and decided to take a long walk. He wandered all around the city. Before he knew it, he had passed outside the walls of London. Soon Tom found himself standing in front of the majestic palace at Westminster. His heart raced with the hope of seeing a real prince!

On each side of the palace gate stood a man-at-arms, clad from head to toe in shiny armor. There were many country folk standing around, also hoping to see a member of the royal family. Splendid carriages and servants passed in and out of the gates.

Poor little Tom, in his rags, moved slowly and timidly past the guards. Suddenly he saw something through the bars that almost made him shout for joy. Within was a handsome boy, whose clothing was made of soft silks and satins and shining with jewels. A little sword and dagger hung from his side. On his head he wore a crimson cap with drooping plumes fastened with a large sparkling gem. He was a prince—a *real* prince. The pauper's wish had been granted.

Tom's eyes grew big with wonder and delight. He wanted to get close to the prince. He pressed his face against the gate bars.

One of the guards noticed and snatched him roughly away from the gate. The soldier said, "Mind your manners, beggar!" Tom went spinning into the crowd. The crowd jeered and laughed.

But the young prince came foward at

once. He cried out, "How dare you treat a poor boy like that? Open the gate and let him in!" The soldiers obeyed.

Edward Tudor, the Prince of Wales, was moved by Tom's hunger and ragged appearance. Edward took Tom to a lavish room inside the palace. A feast, the likes of which Tom had only imagined, was brought in.

The prince sent the servants away so that Tom would not feel uncomfortable. Then Edward asked Tom his name and where he lived. Tom told the prince about his mean grandmother and his scoundrel of a father. The little prince was appalled when he heard about Tom's beatings.

Then Tom told the prince about his kind mother and sisters. Edward also had two sisters.

"Do your sisters forbid their servants to smile, as my older sister does?" Edward asked.

"Servants! My sisters have no servants," Tom said.

"No servants?" Edward asked in amazement. "Who helps them dress and undress?" Edward couldn't believe that people lived without servants and dressed and undressed themselves.

Then Tom told the prince about life in Offal Court. He told amazing stories about racing with friends and good times swimming in the canals.

"It would be worth my father's kingdom to enjoy doing that, even but once!" Edward said.

Then Edward got an idea. Since he wanted to enjoy the life of an ordinary boy for one day and Tom wanted to live like a prince, he decided that they should switch places. Edward suggested that they exchange clothes. When they were done, they realized that they looked exactly alike!

Just then, the prince noticed a bruise on Tom's hand. The guard had done it when he tried to force Tom from the

gate. The prince was outraged.

"It was a cruel thing to do," he said. "Stay here while I take care of the matter. That is a command!"

In a moment he had snatched up and put away an article of national importance that lay upon a table. Then he was out the door and flying through the palace grounds in his rags. As soon as he reached the gate, he shouted, "Open the gates!"

The soldier that had bruised Tom grabbed the prince and threw him out of the palace grounds.

"Stay away, you beggar," the guard shouted. "That will teach you to cause my prince to scold me!" The crowd roared with laughter.

The prince picked himself out of the mud. "I am the Prince of Wales," he yelled. "You will pay for laying your hands upon me!"

"Be gone," the guard called gruffly.

The crowd mocked the little prince as he walked by. "Make way for His Royal Highness!" they scoffed.

# CHAPTER 3

# The Prince's Troubles Begin

After hours of taunting, the crowd finally left the little prince to himself. He looked around but did not recognize his surroundings. All he knew was that he was somewhere in London. He wandered on aimlessly.

As night drew to a close, the prince found himself far down in the close-built portion of the city. He had gotten into many fights that day while trying to convince people that he was the Prince of Wales. His body was bruised, his hands bleeding, and his rags covered with mud. He grew so tired and faint from

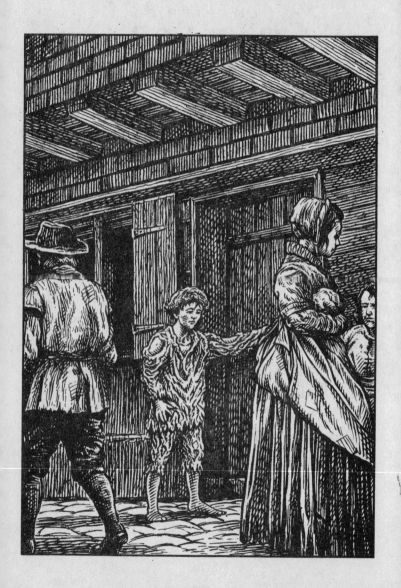

hunger that he could hardly drag one foot after the other.

The prince remembered that Tom had said he was from Offal Court. He thought that if he could just find that place, the Canty family would prove that he was not their son. Then people would believe that he was Edward Tudor. So he set off to find Offal Court.

Suddenly, a rough man grabbed him by his collar. "Out until this time, and not a penny made," the man yelled. "If I

don't break every bone in your body, then I am not John Canty!"

"Oh, so you're his father," the prince said.

"*His* father?" John Canty asked. "I am *your* father, and you are in trouble."

"Oh, delay not," the prince cried. "I am tired and hungry. Take me to my father, the king. He will give you all the money you want."

Canty stared at the boy. "You've gone mad!" he said, grabbing the prince again. "Mad or not, Grandma Canty and I will bring you back to your senses!"

He dragged the frantic, struggling prince away.

## CHAPTER 4

# Tom's Life Changes

Alone in the prince's room, Tom made good use of his opportunity. He looked in the mirror, drew the beautiful sword, and bowed. He kissed the blade and laid it across his breast, as he had seen a knight do. He wondered if his family would believe the tale he would tell when he got home.

After thirty minutes had passed, he suddenly realized that the prince had been gone a long time. He began to feel lonely. He stopped playing with the pretty things around him and grew uneasy and restless.

What if someone came in and saw him wearing the prince's clothes? They

**27**

might arrest him. With these thoughts, his fear grew and grew.

Slowly, he opened the door. Six servants bowed before him. Tom slipped back into the room and shut the door. Then a servant entered and announced, "The Lady Jane Grey."

Tom recognized the name. It was Edward's cousin. Earlier, the prince had told Tom about her.

A young girl entered the room. She was walking toward him when she suddenly stopped. "What ails you, my lord?"

she asked kindly.

"Be merciful," Tom said. "I am not the prince. I am Tom Canty of Offal Court. Please let me see the prince so we can switch our clothes back."

By this time, Tom was on his knees. Jane was horrified that the prince should bow on his knees before her. She ran away in fright.

"Now they will come and take me away," Tom murmured to himself.

After Lady Jane told the story to one person, news quickly spread throughout

the palace. Everyone thought that the prince had gone mad. Soon, the king made an official proclamation. No one was to utter a single word about the prince being insane.

Slowly, poor Tom walked out of the room. He was trembling and bewildered. Soon he found himself in another room. When he looked up, he was staring into the stern face of King Henry VIII!

The king's face grew gentle. He asked, "Edward, why would you try to fool your father with this silly game?" When he saw the look of fear and confusion on

Tom's face, the king believed the rumors of the prince's madness. "Come to your father, son," he said.

The nobles in the room looked concerned. A servant assisted Tom to his feet. He was still trembling as he approached the king. The king took Tom's face between his hands and pressed the boy's head against his chest lovingly.

"You're breaking my heart," the king said sadly, shaking his head. "Don't you know your own father?"

"I beg you to have mercy on me," Tom pleaded. "I was born a pauper. It is only by accident that I am here."

The king assured Tom that nothing bad was going to happen to him. Tom was overjoyed and sprang to his feet. He asked if he would be allowed to go.

"Yes, you may go if you like," the king said. "But why don't you stay a while longer? Where would you go?"

"I thought I was free to go," Tom said.

"I want to go to my humble home. I want to see my mother and sisters."

The king was saddened again by this mad talk from his son. Hopefully, he thought, the prince's wits were sound in other areas. So he asked him a question in Latin. Tom answered him with a blank stare.

"This proves that his mind is diseased," the king said. The court doctor agreed. The king decided to test Tom further and was disappointed when Tom failed to speak to him in French.

"My son is mad, but it is not permanent," the king declared. "Be sure not to strain his mind. Mad or sane, this boy will one day reign!" He ordered that Tom be inducted to his official princely duties as soon as possible.

One of the nobles in the room reminded the king that the Great Marshal of England, the Duke of Norfolk, was in prison in the Tower. The duke had been sentenced to death for treason. Until

another Great Marshal was appointed, there was no one to induct the prince.

"Command Parliament to carry out the duke's sentence before dawn," the king directed. "My son is not to be kept waiting forever."

"You are good to me and I am unworthy," Tom said. "It grieves me to think of that man dying because of me."

"He stands between you and your honor," the king explained. "Do not be troubled by the matter. Go and play. I am not feeling well and must rest."

With a heavy heart, Tom left the room. He knew that he had no hope of being set free. His old dreams had been so pleasant, but being a prince had turned out to be very unpleasant!

# CHAPTER 5
# Tom Learns How to Be a Prince

Tom was led to the main room of a suite, and made to sit down. He didn't want to, since the noblemen around him continued to stand. He begged them to be seated also. They bowed their thanks, but remained standing. He would have insisted, but his "uncle," the Earl of Hertford, whispered in his ear, "It is not proper that they sit in your presence."

Just then, Lord St. John came into the room. He had a special message from the king. He asked Tom to dismiss the others, except for the Earl of Hertford.

Tom did not know what to do. Lord Hertford whispered to him and made a sign with his hand, showing Tom how to dismiss the others.

Then Lord St. John relayed the king's command. Tom was to hide his illness as best as he could, until he was fully cured. He was not to deny that he was the true Prince of Wales. He was to strive to remember all of the people and things that he had forgotten.

At this moment the Lady Elizabeth, the prince's sister, and the Lady Jane Grey were announced. Lord Hertford warned the girls not to act surprised at the prince's memory lapses.

Since there was nothing he could do to change the situation, Tom decided to obey the king's commands.

The conversation between Tom and the young ladies was awkward. Luckily, every time Tom started to say something embarrassing, Lady Elizabeth or Lord Hertford stopped him. Then Lord Hertford suggested that the prince's studies be postponed and he spend his time in more leisurely pursuits.

"What a shame," Lady Jane said. "Don't worry. Soon you will begin your studies again and be able to speak as many languages as your father."

"My father!" cried Tom, off guard for the moment. "Only the swine in kennels can understand his language!" He looked up and saw Lord St. John staring at him. Tom blushed. Lord Hertford explained that the boy's illness had caused his rude behavior.

As time went on, Tom grew more at ease in his new role. The royal family and servants were intent on helping him. The young ladies of the house became Tom's new friends.

Tom was amazed at the number of servants. There were servants to get him a glass of water when he was thirsty and servants to undress him at bedtime.

One night when Tom was in bed, his two guardians discussed his situation.

"What do you make of it?" Lord St. John asked.

"I think that the king is near his end and a mad man will soon reign," Lord Hertford replied.

"It seems strange to me that his madness stripped him of his speech and manners," Lord St. John observed. "It's odd that he completely forgot all of the languages he knew. Maybe he is not the prince, as he said."

"That is treason!" Lord Hertford said. "He looks exactly the same as before. Of course he is the true prince."

# CHAPTER 6
# Tom's First Royal Dinner

In the afternoon, the servants dressed Tom for dinner. Then they led him to a spacious apartment, where a table was set for one. The furniture was made of gold. The room was half-filled with servants. One servant fastened a napkin around Tom's neck. A royal taster stood by, to taste any suspicious dish on command.

An hour earlier, the servants had been instructed to recall that the prince was temporarily out of his mind. They were told not to react to his statements and odd behavior. It made them very sad to see their beloved prince in such a state.

Tom ate with his fingers, but no one smiled or even seemed to notice. He inspected his napkin curiously, "Take it away, before I ruin it," he said.

Tom examined the turnips and the lettuce with interest. He had never seen such food before. He asked what they were, and if they were to be eaten. When he had finished his dessert, he filled his pockets with nuts. No one appeared to notice, but Tom felt that he had done a very unprincely thing.

He didn't have time to worry about it, for his nose began to itch and twitch. His eyes filled with tears as he ran to his guardians. "Please tell me the proper thing to do," Tom cried. "My nose is very itchy. What is the correct procedure for such a situation?"

No one smiled. They all looked at each other for the answer. There was no Royal Nose Scratcher! Meanwhile, tears flowed down Tom's cheeks. Finally, he could no longer bear it, and he scratched his nose himself.

After dinner, a servant held a bowl of rosewater up to Tom. The water was for Tom to clean his hands and mouth. Tom gazed at the dish for a moment or two. Then he raised the bowl to his lips and began to drink the water! The servants pretended not to notice.

At his own request, Tom went back to his room to be alone. Several pieces of a shiny steel armor suit covered with beautiful designs of gold hung from hooks on the wall. This armor belonged to the real prince.

Tom tried on the suit. Then he remembered the nuts he had taken. He thought it would be nice to enjoy them without people watching. So he took the armor off and began to crack the nuts. When he was finished eating, he found a book on the etiquette of the English court. He sat down to read it. This was the first time he had felt happy since he had become a prince.

# CHAPTER 7

# The Great Seal

Late in the afternoon, the king awoke from a nap. He muttered to himself, "What troubling dreams! My end is now at hand! But I will not die until my wish is carried out!"

The Lord Chancellor entered the room. "I have given the order," he said. "The members of Parliament are now awaiting official word from you."

"How long I have waited for this moment," the king said. "I put my Great Seal into effect."

"You gave the Great Seal to the prince two days ago," the Lord Chancellor gently reminded the king. "Shall it be

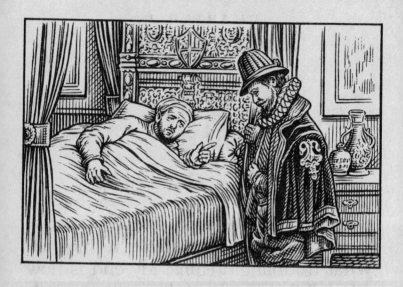

retrieved now?"

The king commanded that the Great Seal be retrieved. Lord Hertford ran off to find Tom. He returned empty-handed. "It hurts me to say so, but the prince's illness remains," Lord Hertford said. "He does not remember anything about the Great Seal. We have searched, but cannot find it."

A groan from the king interrupted the lord. "Trouble the poor child no more," the king said. "Carry out the sentence without the Great Seal! Use the Small Seal instead."

The Lord Chancellor appointed the next day for the Duke of Norfolk to be beheaded. Then he left the room.

A river parade was being held that very night. At nine in the evening, the vast riverfront of the palace was blazing with light. As far as the eye could see, the river's surface was thickly covered with boats, all fringed with colored lanterns. The stone steps leading down to the water were lined with servants, running back and forth. All eyes were on the palace.

Suddenly, trumpets began to blare. Tom stepped onto a high terrace and bowed his head before the people. He was dressed magnificently in a white satin jacket decorated with diamonds and pearls. Born in a hovel, bred in the gutters of London, familiar with rags and dirt and misery, Tom Canty was now quite a spectacle!

## CHAPTER 8
# Prince Edward Meets His New Family

Meanwhile, John Canty was dragging Prince Edward into Offal Court with a noisy mob at their heels. At least one person in the crowd was trying to save the prince from Canty.

The prince struggled for freedom. Canty lost his patience and lifted his club to strike the prince. Then someone sprang up to stop Canty.

"Want to meddle, do you?" Canty roared. "Well, here's what you get for it." With that, he gave the man a crashing blow to the head. The man fell sensless among the feet of the crowd.

The next thing the prince knew, he was in the Canty home. By the dim light of a candle, the prince saw two girls and a middle-aged woman cowering in the corner. A gray-haired old woman with mean eyes sat in another corner, scowling.

"Tell everyone your name," Canty ordered the prince.

"I am Edward, Prince of Wales," the prince replied.

The old woman stared at the prince in amazement. Tom's mothers and sisters ran to comfort him. "Oh, Tom, you poor lad," they cried. Tom's mother fell to her knees before the prince. They thought that Tom had gone mad!

"Your son has not lost his wits," the prince said, trying to comfort Tom's mother. "If you would allow me to go back to my palace, the king, my father, will return Tom to you."

"Please, Tom, try to remember me," Mrs. Canty begged. "I am your own mother."

"I don't want to hurt you madam, but

I have never seen you before," the prince said. Mrs. Canty sobbed.

Tom's father was very amused by the scene. "Nan, Bet, you mannerless girls," he said. "How dare you not bow before the prince." He laughed at his own joke.

The girls were worried about their brother. They begged their father to let the boy go to sleep and promised that he would not come home empty-handed again.

Then the family went to bed. As soon as they heard Canty and the old woman

snoring, the girls crept over to where the prince lay awake. They covered him with straw and rags. Their mother joined them and cried over him. The prince told Mrs. Canty that he would not forget her great kindness. His father, the king would reward her.

As Mrs. Canty tried to fall back to sleep, she couldn't help thinking that there was something about this boy that was different than her son. For a minute, the thought crossed her mind that, perhaps, this was not really Tom, but she dismissed it.

Soon, the prince was sound asleep. He dreamed that he had become a pauper. When he awoke, he realized that it was not a dream.

Suddenly he heard a commotion outside the house. Then someone knocked on the door.

"What do you want?" John Canty shouted.

"Do you know who it was you hit with

your club?" a voice asked.

"I don't know, and I don't care," Canty replied.

"It was the priest, Father Andrew," the voice said. "You killed him."

Canty was alarmed. He woke up his family and ordered everyone to leave the apartment at once. They had to flee before Canty was caught and sent to jail. Soon they were all in the street running for their lives.

Canty grabbed the prince by the wrist

and warned him not to speak. Canty knew he would have to come up with a new name for the family so that they would not be discovered.

"If we get separated, meet at London Bridge," Canty told his family.

At that moment, the family burst out of darkness into a blaze of light. They had run right into the river parade. There were bonfires as far as the eye could see. London Bridge was illuminated. Explosions and sparks from fireworks surrounded them.

The Cantys were swallowed by the crowd. Canty kept a firm grip on the prince, but the rest of the family was separated from each other.

The prince realized that the celebration was in his honor. He concluded that Tom had deliberately taken advantage of the opportunity to take his place as Prince of Wales. So he broke away from Canty and vowed to return to the palace to reclaim his title.

# CHAPTER 9

# At Guildhall

Attended by its gorgeous fleet, the royal barge sailed down the Thames River through the wilderness of illuminated boats. The air was filled with music. The distant city lay in a soft glow cast by countless bonfires.

To Tom Canty, half buried in his silk cushions, this spectacle was a wonder. To the young friends at his side, the Princess Elizabeth and the Lady Jane Grey, it was not so extraordinary.

When the barge came to a halt in London, Tom disembarked. Then he and his gallant procession made a short march to Guildhall.

Tom and his friends were received with due ceremony by the Lord Mayor and the Fathers of the City, who sat together in front of the hall in their gold chains and scarlet robes. At a lower table, the other guests of noble degree were seated. The commoners took places at a multitude of tables on the main floor of the hall.

Tom was instructed to raise his cup and take a sip. Then he passed the cup to Lady Elizabeth, who passed it to Lady Jane. Thus, the banquet began.

By midnight the celebration was at its height. The minstrels played merry tunes. The lords and ladies danced. From his seat, Tom gazed at the dancing. He was dazzled by the swirling colors.

Meanwhile, the ragged little Prince of Wales stood at the gates of Guildhall, proclaiming his rights and denouncing the impostor. The crowd pressed forward to see the small rioter. They began to

taunt and mock him.

"Prince or no prince, you are not friendless," a man called gallantly from the crowd. "I will stand by your side. You could have no better friend than Miles Hendon."

The speaker was tall and muscular. His clothes were made of fine materials, but were faded and threadbare. The plume in his slouched hat was broken. A rusty sword hung at his side.

The crowd met his speech with laughter. Someone cried, "It's another prince in disguise!"

Then someone grabbed the prince. Miles drew his sword and knocked the man to the ground. Instantly, the mob closed in on him. Luckily, a trumpet sounded and a horse carrying the king's messenger broke through the crowd. Miles scooped up the prince and ran.

Inside Guildhall, everyone grew quiet. The messenger declared, "The king is dead!"

The company bowed their heads. Then they turned their eyes on Tom and

shouted, "The king is dead. Long live the king!" Tom was now the King of England!

"The king's law will be a law of mercy and never more a law of blood," Tom declared. "I decree that the Duke of Norfolk will not die!"

The crowd yelled, "The reign of blood is ended! Long live Edward, King of England!"

# CHAPTER 10

# Miles Hendon to the Rescue

As soon as Miles Hendon and the little prince, who was now a king, were clear of the mob, they headed toward the river. Edward learned of his father's death from the yells of the crowds. He was filled with grief, but determined to take his rightful place as king.

Miles and the king slowly crossed the bridge. Closely packed stores, with family quarters overhead, lined the bridge on either side. Miles' lodgings were in the little inn on the bridge. As he neared the door with his young friend, a rough voice said, "You won't escape again! If you do, I'll pound you!" It was John Canty. He

put his hand out to seize the boy, but Miles stopped him.

"Who are you?" Miles demanded.

"I am this boy's father, not that it's your business," Canty said.

"That's a lie," cried the king. "I will die before I go with him."

"I saved him from an angry mob," Miles said. "And I will not let him go to a worse fate." Miles drew his sword.

Canty moved off, muttering threats. He disappeared into the crowd.

Miles and the king walked into the inn. Miles' apartment was shabby, with only a bed and a few pieces of furniture in it. Immediately, the king climbed into bed. He was exhausted. "Call me when the table is spread," he said.

Miles smiled and noted how easily the little beggar made himself at home and ordered Miles around. He was amazed at how well the boy kept playing the part of a prince. He decided to be the boy's friend and act as a big brother to him.

Just then, the boy shivered. Miles had no extra blankets to give him, so he took the shirt off of his back and wrapped the king in it.

"If my father is still alive," Miles said to himself, "he will surely take the poor lad in, for my sake."

A servant entered with a hot meal and slammed the door, waking the king. The prince saw that he was wrapped in Miles' shirt. He vowed to repay Miles' kindness when his identity was proven.

The king walked to the washstand

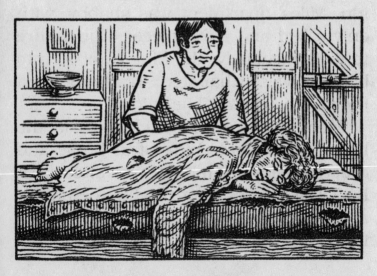

and stood there. When Miles asked what was wrong, he said that he would like to wash before dinner. Miles told him to wash himself as he pleased, but the king impatiently tapped his foot. "You don't expect the king to wash himself, do you?" the boy asked. "Come and pour the water."

Miles had to hold back his laughter. It amused him to see the boy carry on the silly charade. To play along, he did as he was told.

But when Miles was about to sit down at the table, the king cried out, "Hold! Would you sit in the presence of the king?"

So Miles removed the chair and stood while they ate, waiting on the king as he could.

As they ate, the boy said, "You have a noble air about you. Were you born into the nobility?"

"My father is a baronet, Sir Richard Hendon of Hendon Hall," Miles

explained. "He is very rich. My older brother, Arthur, is a kind soul like my father. My younger brother, Hugh, is very mean and underhanded. I love the Lady Edith, but she was betrothed to Arthur from birth. Even though Arthur loved another woman, my father would not hear of breaking the engagement.

"One day, Hugh convinced my father that I planned to elope with Lady Edith. My father sent me off to be a soldier, thinking that it would be good for me. I was taken captive in the last battle. I have been imprisoned in a dungeon for the past seven years."

The king was moved by the story Miles told him. He thought for a moment, then said, "You have been wronged. As the King of England, I will right these wrongs!" Then he told Miles how he had come to be mistaken for a pauper.

When he finished, Miles said to himself, "What an imagination he has!"

"You saved my life," the boy said. "Name your desire and it shall be granted."

Miles played along with the king. He got down upon one knee. He said, "But since you would like to reward me, I will ask you for one wish, that I, and all of my successors, be allowed to forever *sit* in the presence of the king."

"Rise, Sir Miles Hendon, Knight," said the king. "Your petition is granted."

Miles was noticeably relieved. He much preferred to *sit* in the king's presence, than to *stand!*

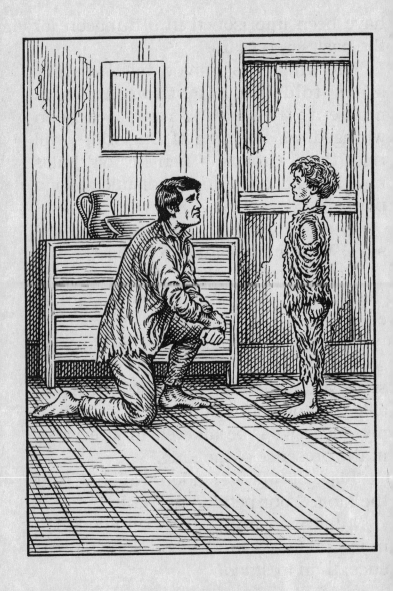

# CHAPTER 11

# The King Disappears

Soon it was time for the two friends to go to sleep. The king took Miles' bed. He ordered Miles to sleep near the door, to guard it.

The next morning, Miles awoke first. While the king was still asleep, Miles took his measurements and quietly slipped out. He returned with a second-hand suit for the boy. The material was cheap, but it was clean and neat. With the little money he had left, Miles planned to buy donkeys to take them on the long journey to Hendon Hall.

When he went to wake the boy, Miles realized that the king was gone!

Immediately, Miles went to the door. He was met by a servant, who had come to clean the apartment.

"Where is the boy?" Miles asked.

"While you were gone, a young man came by," the servant explained. "He said that you sent him to get the boy and bring him to you."

"You are a fool and were easily fooled!" Miles yelled. "I hope that no harm has been done to him. Tell me, was this young man alone?"

"Yes, I am sure that he was," the servant replied. "No, now I remember that as the two reached the bridge, a rough-looking man joined them."

Miles thought that it must have been John Canty who had met them. Alarmed, Miles ran off to find them.

\*\*\*

Meanwhile, at dawn, Tom stirred out of a heavy sleep and opened his eyes in the dark. For a moment, he thought that everything that had happened had been a dream. He called out for his sisters.

But it was Lord Hertford who came to him. Then he knew it was all very real. The room was filled with lords and servants. He rose and went through the complicated process of being dressed by the servants.

After breakfast, Tom was conducted ceremoniously to the throne room, where he was expected to transact business of state. Lord Hertford took his side by the throne, to assist Tom with wise

counsel.

One of the points of business was the former king's debts. He owed wages to many of the servants. Tom suggested that the court move into smaller quarters that cost less money. Lord Hertford pinched his arm to alert him that his answer was inappropriate.

Tom found the work to be dull. Many petitions were read. Tom wished that he were back in the fields, playing and laughing with his friends.

During the afternoon, Tom spent an enjoyable hour with Lady Elizabeth and Lady Jane. Then a skinny boy was brought into the room. He came forward, and kneeled before Tom.

"Rise," Tom said. "Who are you?"

"Surely you must remember me," the boy said. "I am your whipping boy, Humphrey Marlow."

Tom thought that this was someone his guardians should have told him about. He wondered if he should pretend to know the boy.

"I seem to remember you, somewhat," Tom lied. "Give me some clues to refresh my memory."

"Do you remember a few days ago, when you made three mistakes in your Greek lesson?" Humphrey asked.

"I think so," Tom said.

"The master was angry at your laziness. He promised that he would whip me for it," Humphrey said.

"Whip *you*, for my mistakes?" Tom asked increduously.

"I always get whipped when you fail at your lessons," Humphrey said. "The Prince of Wales must not be touched. It is my job to take your blows."

"I will see to it that you never get whipped again," Tom said.

"Thank you, my good king!" cried the boy, dropping to his knees. "I do not mean to seem ungrateful, but something troubles me. Since you are no longer having your lessons, I am not needed. I will not have a job, and my orphan sisters and I will starve."

Tom was touched by Humphrey's distress. "Your position shall be permanent for you and your family forever," Tom said. "But you will *not* be whipped."

"Thank you, most noble master," Humphrey cried.

Tom asked the boy to stay for a while. He thought that talking to Humphrey might give him more information about the prince's life. After an hour, Tom had discovered much about Prince Edward's daily routine.

As Humphrey was leaving, Lord Hertford arrived to announce that word had spread about the king's "madness." Lord Hertford said it would be best for Tom to dine in public twice a week to show his subjects that he was fit to rule over the kingdom.

# CHAPTER 12

# Tom Ascends to the Throne

The next day, the foreign ambassadors came to the king's palace. Lord Hertford told Tom what to say and how to act. Tom looked like a king, although he did not feel like one. He was very glad when the event was over.

On the fourth day of Tom's kingship, he was scheduled to dine in public. He dreaded it. He looked out of a window, and longed to be a part of life outside the castle once again. At that moment, he heard a mob yelling outside.

Lord Hertford sent a page to investigate. When the page returned, he said that the crowd was following a man who

was to be executed.

Tom was alarmed by this news. "Bring the man here," he ordered.

In a little while, the criminal was brought before him. Something about the man stirred a memory in Tom. Then he remembered that this man had saved Tom's friend, Giles, from drowning in the river that past summer. Tom learned that the man had been accused of poisoning someone to death.

"Please have pity on me," the man said. "I have been falsely accused. Please

do not let them boil me alive!"

"Even if you had poisoned a hundred men, I would not wish such a horrible punishment on you," Tom said. At once, Tom ordered that such punishment be carried out no more in England.

After Tom heard the man's full story, he said, "But no poison was found and none was seen given." He wasn't convinced that there was enough evidence against the man.

"I am afraid that there is nothing I can say that will save me," the man said. "But on that very day I saved a boy from drowning."

Tom asked the man when it had happened. When he heard the answer, Tom knew for sure that it was the same man who had saved his friend. Tom ordered that the man be set free.

A low buzz of admiration swept through the assembly. People were convinced that the new king was wise and fit to rule over them.

The dinner hour drew near, but the morning's events had given Tom such confidence that he was not nervous about eating dinner before the public.

The banquet room was very large, with gilded pillars all around. Tom's table was in the center of the room on a raised platform.

Down the echoing corridors, calls of "Make way for the king!" could be heard. Then a parade of gentleman, barons, earls, knights, and chancellors, all richly dressed, filed into the hall.

Tom carried himself with great dignity. He greeted everyone with a courteous, "Thank you, my good people." Then he seated himself at his table.

Although Tom was well aware that all eyes were on him, he performed very well at dinner. He made it through the entire evening without making one mistake. It was a flawless triumph.

# CHAPTER 13

# Foo-foo the First

The ruffian walked closely behind Edward and the young man as they crossed the bridge. He wore a patch over one eye, and his arm was in a sling.

The young man led the king on a crooked course through Southwark. The king became more and more irritated. He felt that it was Miles' place to come to him, not the other way around. The king stopped and said, *"I must rest."*

"Do you really want to stop here when your friend is lying wounded in the woods?" the young man asked.

"Wounded?" asked the king. "Who dared to do it? The scoundrel will be sorry for wounding him."

They went quite a distance through the woods, but the young man and the king traveled at a fast pace. Soon they reached a clearing with a deserted barn nearby. The young man entered the barn, and the king followed.

The king looked around for Miles. "Where is he?" he asked.

His question was answered with a mocking laugh from the ruffian who had been following them. The king was enraged.

"Who are you and what is your business here?" the king asked.

"My disguise is not so good that you don't recognize your own father, is it?" the ruffian asked. It was John Canty!

"You are not my father," the king cried. "My father is dead, and now I am the king. If you have hidden my servant, Miles, you shall pay dearly."

"It is plain to see that you are mad," John Canty said. "Your threats do not frighten me. I have committed a murder and cannot go back home. From now on, I am John Hobbs. You will be known as Jack. Where are your mother and sisters? Why have they not come to the appointed place?"

"My mother is dead, and my sisters are at the palace," the king replied.

The young man who was with them burst into laughter.

"Hugo, do not tease him," Canty said. "His mind is not well. Sit down, Jack."

While Hugo and Canty stood together

talking, the king walked into the barn. At the far end, he found a pile of straw and sat down to rest. He thought about his real father and began to cry. Soon, he was fast asleep.

After quite some time, the king was awakened by the sound of rain beating on the roof. Then a chorus of loud cackles and coarse laughter startled him. He looked around and saw a sight that terrified him. A huge fire blazed on the other side of the barn. Around it danced the oddest bunch of characters that the

king had ever seen. There were huge men and young boys dressed in rags. There were blind beggars with patches covering their eyes, crippled and diseased men with sores all over their bodies, and foul-mouthed women of all ages.

From what the king observed, "John Hobbs" was not new to the group. When Hobbs reported how he had killed Father Andrew, the group cheered.

When Hobbs asked how many people were now in the group, the chief answered that there were twenty-five people. Others had already moved east for the winter. The rest planned to follow in the morning.

"Have any of our friends fallen on hard times?" Hobbs asked.

"Yes," the chief answered. "Some of the newcomers had their farms taken away. The farms were converted into sheep ranges. They had no choice but to beg. Then they were whipped and beaten for begging. After they were captured, they were sold as slaves."

The chief asked some of the men to show Hobbs their scars. One man had had an ear cut off.

Another man, named Yokel, stood to tell his story. He had been a prosperous farmer with a wife and children. His farm was taken and his family eventually starved to death. Since it was a crime to beg in England, Yokel was sold into slavery. He had been running from his master for many months. If caught, he would be hanged.

"You will not be hanged!" a voice called out. "That law ends on this day!"

They all turned to see who was speaking. It was the king. He was hurrying toward them. Everyone wanted to know who this strange boy was.

"I am Edward, king of England," the king said with dignity.

A burst of laughter rang out. Everyone thought the boy's speech was an excellent joke.

"You mannerless vagrants," the king cried. "Is this how you show your gratitude to me?" He tried to say more, but his voice was drowned by the whirlwind of laughter.

At last Hobbs was able to yell above the noise of the crowd. "Quiet down, you rowdy bunch! Mates, the boy is my son," he said. "He is a dreamer and a fool. Do not mind him. He thinks he is the king."

"I do not think it," Edward said. "I *am* the king. You will find out the truth in good time. Hobbs, you are a confessed murderer. You will pay dearly."

"You would betray your own father?" Hobbs asked. "I should let this crowd have their sport with you! Just wait until I get my hands on you!"

"Stop," the chief said, stepping between the king and Hobbs just in time. He knocked Hobbs down. "Have you no respect for kings or chiefs?" he asked. He turned to the king and said, "Pretend to be king, if it pleases you, but do not make threats against my friends, lad. Now, all together, repeat after me, "Long live Edward, King of England!"

"Long live Edward, King of England!" the crowd cheered.

The king's face lit up with pleasure. "I thank you, my good people," he said.

The gang roared with laughter. The chief told Edward that he could believe that he was anyone, but told the boy to call himself by another name so people would not think he was mad.

One of the men suggested "Foo-foo the First." Everyone started hailing the boy by this new name.

Before he knew it, Edward was robed in a tattered blanket and seated on a barrel throne. The revelers flung themselves at his knees in mockery. The chief bowed low to the ground and kissed the boy's feet.

## CHAPTER 14
# A Merry Band

At dawn, the troop of vagabonds set out toward the east. There was a cloudy sky overhead, muddy ground under foot, and a winter chill in the air. All were sullen, silent and irritable.

The chief put Edward in Hugo's care for the journey. He told Hugo not to treat the boy roughly. He warned Hobbs to stay away from the boy.

After a while, the weather grew milder, and the clouds lifted somewhat. The troop grew more and more cheerful and began to enjoy insulting passengers along the highway.

Soon they came to a small farmhouse and made themselves at home. The farmer and his family, fearful of their threats, made breakfast for them. When they left, the vagabonds warned the family that they would burn down the house if the family reported them.

After a long and weary voyage, the troop stopped behind a hedge on the outskirts of a village. They rested there for an hour. Then the troop scattered to enter the village at different points. Edward was sent with Hugo.

They wandered about for some time as Hugo looked for good begging opportunities.

"I will not beg!" the king declared.

"You beg all the time in London!" Hugo exclaimed, eyeing the king with surprise.

"You are tiring me," the king said.

"Fine, you will not beg or steal," Hugo said. "But you will play decoy while I beg. If you refuse you'll pay for it."

Just then Hugo saw a man with a kind face approaching. Hugo said he

would fall down in a mock fit. When the stranger approached, Edward was supposed to say that Hugo was his brother and that they were homeless and friendless. Then Hugo would beg the man for money.

Hugo began to moan and groan. He rolled his eyes and began to wobble from side to side. When the stranger came near, Hugo shrieked.

"Oh, dear!" cried the kind stranger. "Oh, poor soul. Let me help you."

"Could you please spare a penny for me and my brother, dear sir, to buy a little food?" Hugo asked.

"I will give you three pennies, you poor creatures," the man said. Then he turned to the king. "Come here and help me carry your brother, little boy."

"He is not my brother," said the king.

"If he is not your brother, then who is he?" the stranger asked Hugo.

"A beggar and a thief!" Edward cried. "He has got your money and has picked your pocket, too."

Hugo did not wait to see the man's reaction. In a moment, he was up and running. The gentleman ran after him.

The terrified king fled in the opposite direction as fast as he could, looking over his shoulder to see if he was being followed. He did not slow down until he was sure he was out of harm's way.

Night was falling. but the king kept moving. Every time he stopped, he was overcome by the cold.

Finally, he came to an empty barn. He waited outside for a long time, but saw no one enter or exit the barn. Then he decided to go in.

The king spotted a pile of blankets in the corner of the barn. Although the king was hungry and cold, he was also tired. Soon he dozed off.

Suddenly, he felt something touch him. He lay motionless and listened, hardly breathing.

The king summoned all of his courage

and reached further and further until his hand swept against something furry and warm. It was a calf!

The king was ashamed of himself for being afraid of a harmless animal! Happily, he drifted off to sleep with the calf sleeping next to him.

# CHAPTER 15
# The Prince
# and the Hermit

Early the next morning, the king was awakened by the sound of the farm workers arriving to do their duties. Edward was very frightened. He did not want to be discovered, so he crept out of the barn and ran down the road. He never looked back until he had come to the shelter of the forest.

He ran through the cold, dark forest, hoping to reach a road. He traveled on and on, but the further he went, the denser the woods became. Before he knew it, the king realized that night was falling. He tried to run faster, but he kept getting tangled in vines and roots.

How glad he was when at last he saw a glimmer of light. He stepped toward it warily, stopping to look around him and listen. The light came from the window of a shabby little hut.

He heard a voice and started to run away. Then he changed his mind and stepped closer to the hut. He tiptoed up to the window and glanced inside.

Before an altar, a single candle was lit. An old man knelt in front of it. On a wooden box in front of him was an open book and a human skull. The man was

tall and very bony. His hair and beard were very long and snowy white. He wore a robe of sheepskin, which reached from his neck to his heels.

"How fortunate I am," the king said to himself. "I have found a holy hermit!"

When the hermit rose from his knees, the king knocked on the door. A deep voice responded, "Enter! But leave evil doing behind, for the ground whereon you shall stand is holy!"

The king entered and looked around.

The room was very small. In the corner was a small bed with a ragged blanket. There was a little bench and a three-legged stool as well. The hermit turned a pair of suspicious eyes on him. He said, "Who are you?"

"I am the king," he answered.

"Welcome, King!" cried the hermit with enthusiasm. Happily, he arranged the bench for the king to sit on. Then he started pacing the floor nervously.

"Many have sought sanctuary here,"

the man said. "But none have been so worthy as a king, and they were turned away. A king who casts off his crown, dresses in rags, and devotes his life to goodness is welcome."

The king tried to explain his situation, but the hermit would not give the boy a chance. He continued, "You shall be at peace here. No one will find out where you are or take you back to your worldly life. Here you will live simply."

Finally, the old man stopped speaking. He started to pace back and forth again. The king took this opportunity to tell the man the truth. But the hermit went on muttering and paid no heed.

"Be quiet. I want to tell you a secret," the old man said. He bent down. He made sure that there was no one outside the window who could hear. Then he whispered, "I am an archangel!"

The king became very nervous. *Oh, how I wish that I were with the outlaws again*, he thought. *Now I am the prisoner of a madman.* His fear showed plainly on his face.

"There's an expression of awe on your face," said the old man. "It is true. I was made an archangel on this very spot, five years ago."

He chattered on for an hour. The king sat and suffered through his babble. Then the hermit's voice softened. The old man dressed the boy's cuts and bruises. He cooked him a hearty supper, chatting merrily the whole time. Occasionally, he patted the boy's head.

After dinner, the hermit tucked the boy into bed. The old man said, "So, what are you the king of?"

"Of England," Edward replied.

"Of England? Then Henry is gone?" the man asked.

"Yes, I am his son," the king replied.

The hermit frowned. He clenched his bony hands. He stood still for a few moments, breathing fast and swallowing. Then he said, "Do you know that

good King Henry turned us out into the world, homeless and poor?"

The king was silent. The old man bent down and listened to his breathing. The boy was fast asleep.

"Your father ruined us," the hermit whispered. "He destroyed us."

The old man walked back and forth across his small hut gathering rags. He tied the king's ankles together without waking the boy. Then he gagged and bound the boy's wrists. The king slept peacefully through it all.

CHAPTER 16

# Miles to the Rescue, Again!

The old man pulled up the bench and sat in front of the sleeping king. He kept an eye on the boy, as he slowly rubbed his hands and chuckled to himself.

After a very long time, the man noticed that the boy's eyes were wide open! The king stared in terror at the old man. His little body trembled and struggled against the bindings.

The old man smiled. "Have you said your final prayers, son of King Henry?" he asked.

The boy tried to make a sound but could not. He tried again and managed to force a smothered sound through his closed jaws. The hermit took this as a positive answer to his question.

"Then pray again," the hermit snarled. "Pray your final prayers!"

A shudder shook the boy's frame. His face turned pale. Then he struggled again to free himself, turning and twisting himself, this way and that. He tugged frantically, fiercely, desperately— but uselessly—to loosen the ropes. All the while, the old man rubbed his hands.

From time to time, the old man mumbled, "Your moments are precious and few, little king."

Finally, the boy uttered a defeated groan and stopped struggling. He was panting. Tears streamed heavily down his anxious face.

Dawn was beginning to break. The old man spoke sharply, with a touch of nervousness in his voice. "The night is already done. How quickly it has gone!"

The rest of his speech consisted of mumbles, which the king did not understand.

The old man sank upon his knees and bent over the groaning boy. Suddenly, they heard voices outside the cabin. The old man was startled and stopped rubbing his hands. He threw a sheepskin over the boy and got up off of the floor. He was trembling.

The sounds outside grew louder and became rough and angry. Then they heard the clatter of approaching footsteps. Someone knocked roughly on the cabin door.

"Open up," a voice called.

This was the sweetest sound that the king could possibly hear. It was Miles Hendon's voice!

Grinding his teeth in a violent rage, the hermit moved quickly away from the bed and left the room, closing the door behind him. The king could hear a heated conversation taking place in the other room.

"Where is the boy?" Miles demanded. He was furious.

"What boy?" the old man asked.

"Tell me no lies, sir," Miles demanded. "Very near here, I caught the scoundrels who stole him from me. I made them confess, and they told me the boy was missing again. They had tracked him to your door. They showed me his foot-prints. Now tell me, where is he?"

"Oh, you mean the ragged royal vagrant that spent the night here," the

hermit said. "I have sent him on an errand. He will be back very soon."

"Do not waste my time. How soon will he be back?" Miles asked. Do you think that I can catch up to him?"

"Do not worry, sir," the hermit said. "He will be back soon."

"Then I will remain here until he returns," Miles said. "Wait! You sent him on an errand? It is a lie! He would not have taken orders from the likes of you, or from any man."

"From any man, no," the hermit replied. "But I am no ordinary man. I am an archangel."

Miles laughed. "He would obey no mere mortal," Miles said. "But even a king must obey an archangel! Shh—what was that noise?"

Although Miles did not know it, the king had been in the next room all that time. One moment he trembled with fear. The next, he quaked with hope. He had been trying to moan as loudly as he

could, hoping that Miles would hear him and come to the rescue.

"What noise?" the hermit asked. "I only heard the wind."

"I just heard it again," Miles said. "It is not the wind."

The king was overjoyed, but his heart sank when he heard the hermit say, "It came from outside. Let's investigate. I will lead the way."

The king heard the men leave the hut. The sound of their footsteps quickly faded away. He was alone in an awful silence. It seemed like an eternity before he heard footsteps returning. This time, he also heard the trample of hooves.

"I cannot wait any longer," Miles said. "He has lost his way and is in danger."

"I will go with you," the hermit said.

"Maybe you are better than you look," Miles said. "Take the boy's donkey." Then they rode off.

The king lost all hope. *My only friend has been deceived and is now gone*, he thought. Frantically, he shook the sheepskin off.

Then he heard the door open again!

The creaking of the hinges chilled him to the bone. The horror of it all forced him to close his eyes. When he opened them, he saw John Canty and Hugo standing before him.

A moment later, King Edward was free. Then his captors, each gripping him by an arm, hurried him through the forest.

# CHAPTER 17
# A Victim of Treachery

Once again King Foo-foo the First was roving with the band of outlaws and the butt of their jokes. Sometimes when the chief's back was turned, Canty and Hugo hit the boy. Still, with the exception of Hugo and Canty, everyone liked him. They admired his strong spirit.

At night the outlaws danced and sang around a bonfire. Twice, Hugo "accidentally" stepped on Edward's toes. The third time he tried to do this, the king knocked him to the ground with a club. This delighted the gang. Embarrassed and angry, Hugo charged toward the boy, but he was no match for the coura-

geous king, who soundly beat his opponent. The crowd cheered and dubbed Edward "King of the Gamers."

All attempts to make Edward join their robbing and begging had failed. Once, when he had been forced into a house to rob it, not only did he emerge empty-handed, but he also tried to wake the inhabitants to warn them. After that, Hugo was put in charge of keeping the king from escaping.

Each night, in the king's dreams, he forgot the weariness of his new life. He was on his throne, and master again. But the relief he felt in his dreams only intensified the sufferings of his new life.

Hugo wanted to get back at the king for humiliating him. Since he could not humiliate the king, he decided to set the king up to look like a criminal.

One afternoon, Hugo decided to put his plan to work. He strolled off to a neighboring village with Edward. As they walked up and down one street, Hugo looked for a chance to achieve his wicked purpose, and the king looked for an opportunity to escape.

Hugo's chance came when a woman approached. She carried a large package in a basket.

"Wait here until I come back," Hugo said, darting after the woman.

The king was filled with joy. He thought that he could escape, if only Hugo would wander far enough away.

He was to have no such luck. Hugo crept behind the woman, snatched the package, and came running back. He

wrapped it in an old blanket, which he carried on his arm. The woman screamed, but she had not seen Hugo before he ran away. When he reached the king, Hugo thrust the bundle into the boy's hand and took off.

Hugo turned a corner and darted down a crooked alley. In a few minutes, he emerged, looking innocent. He stopped to watch the results of his actions.

The insulted king threw the bundle on the ground. The blanket fell away from it just as the woman arrived, with a growing crowd at her heels. She seized the king's wrist with one hand, snatched her bundle with the other, and yelled at the boy while he struggled.

Hugo had seen enough. His enemy had been captured. So he slipped away, happy and chuckling.

The king continued to struggle. "Unhand me, you foolish woman," he cried. "I am not a thief."

The crowd closed in, threatening the king and calling him names. Just then, a sword flashed through the air, parting the angry crowd.

"This is a matter for the law, not for a mob," Miles said. "Loosen your grip, woman!"

The woman let go of Edward's wrist. The crowd quieted down.

The king ran to his rescuer. "It has taken you a long while, but you came right in the nick of time," he said. "Thank you, Sir Miles!"

# CHAPTER 18

# The Prince Becomes a Prisoner

Miles held back a smile. He bent down and whispered into the king's ear, "Be quiet now, my king. Trust in me and all will go well in the end."

An officer approached. He was about to seize the king, but Miles said, "There is no need to force him. He will go peacefully, on his own. Lead on, and we will follow."

The officer led the way. The woman and her bundle followed closely behind. The crowd followed at their heels.

When the woman was called to testify before the judge, she swore that Edward was the person who had stolen her goods. There was no one able to testify to his innocence, so the king stood convicted. The bundle was unrolled. It contained a plump little pig.

The judge asked the woman what the pig was worth. The woman told the judge that she had paid three shillings for it. The judge ordered that the court be cleared and the doors shut.

"Perhaps the boy was starving," the judge said. "When one is starving, desperate measures are sometimes taken. Do you know that the penalty for stealing something worth more than two shillings is hanging?"

The king was startled, but he remained calm. The woman said she did not know the penalty was so severe. She sprang to her feet, shaking with fright.

"What have I done?" she cried. "I do not want him to die. What can I do?"

"The best thing to do is reconsider the value of the pig," the judge said.

"Then I say that the pig is worth one

shilling," the woman announced.

Miles was delighted. He threw his arms around the surprised king and hugged him. The grateful woman grabbed her pig and walked out of the room. One of the officers followed her out into the hallway.

"That is a fine pig," the officer said. "I will pay you one shilling for it."

"One shilling!" the woman cried. "You'll do no such thing. I paid three shillings for it."

"But you swore under oath that it was worth one shilling," the officer said. "You lied. Come back to the judge with me and report your crime. Then the lad will hang."

"Say no more," the woman replied. "Give me the shilling and we'll be done."

The woman ran off crying. Miles had witnessed the entire incident.

The judge lectured the king on the perils of stealing. He sentenced Edward to a short stay in jail. The king opened

his mouth to reprimand the judge, but Miles stopped him. Miles took him by the hand and they marched off toward the jail, led by the officer.

"Do you think I will enter a common jail willingly?" the king asked.

"Please trust me," Miles said. "Be patient. I will take care of the matter."

## CHAPTER 19
# Hendon Hall

Soon the king and his party arrived at a deserted market square and proceeded to cross it. When they had reached the middle of it, Miles touched Edward's arm. He said, in a low voice, "Wait a moment, sir. I would like to have a word with the officer."

Miles turned to the officer. "Let the poor lad escape," he said.

"My duty forbids it," the officer replied.

"The pig that you got for a shilling may cost you your neck," Miles said.

At first, the officer was speechless. Then the officer threatened Miles, who told the officer that he had heard every word the officer had said to the woman. Miles threatened to tell the judge.

"Escape with the lad," the officer cried angrily. "I will say the prisoner broke away."

So Miles and the king escaped!

As soon as Miles and the king were out of the officer's sight, Miles instructed the boy to hurry to a certain spot outside of town. Then Miles went to settle his account at the inn.

Thirty minutes later, the two friends met and headed eastward. The king was now wearing the second-hand suit that Miles had bought for him.

Miles wanted nothing more than to get back to the home he missed so much. But he thought that a speedy journey would be hard on the boy, so they made the trip in short stages, stopping whenever the king grew tired.

For two days they moved lazily along, talking about the adventures each had

had during the time they were apart. Miles told Edward that the hermit went into the bedroom and emerged looking broken-hearted because he had expected to find the boy still there.

Then Edward told of how the old man tied him up and meant to harm him. When Miles heard that, he was sorry that he did not thrash the archangel when he had had the chance.

During the last day of the trip, Miles' spirits soared. He talked about his father, his brother Arthur, and his beloved Lady Edith. He was even able to say some gentle things about Hugh. He talked about what a surprise his return would be to everybody, and what an outburst of delight there would be.

They traveled through a fair region, dotted with cottages and orchards. The road led through broad green pastures. At last, Miles cried, "There is the village, my king, and there is Hendon Hall! You can see the towers from here."

They hurried as fast as they could. It

was afternoon by the time they reached the village. The friends scampered through it, Miles pointing out the places and people he remembered so well.

"There is the church, and there is the Red Lion Inn," he said. "Nothing has changed, except for the people. No one seems to know me."

When they reached the end of the village, Miles and the king went down a narrow road, which was walled in with hedges. Then they passed through a vast flower garden and a gateway. A stately mansion was in front of them.

"Welcome to Hendon Hall, my king!" Miles exclaimed. "This is a great day. My family will be so happy to see us."

The next moment Miles rushed into the mansion, holding the king by the hand. They stepped into a very large room with fine furnishings. Miles ran toward a man who was sitting at a writing table in front of a large fire.

"I am back, Hugh!" Miles cried. "Call

Father, for home is not home until I see his face and hear his voice!"

Hugh drew back and stared gravely at the intruder. He said, "Your mind seems to be touched, stranger. You must have suffered in this cruel world. Who do you think I am?"

"You are my brother, Hugh Hendon," Miles replied.

"And who do you imagine yourself to be?" Hugh asked.

"Imagination has nothing to do with it," Miles said. "Why are you pretending not to know your own brother, Miles Hendon?"

"You are not joking," Hugh said. "Can the dead come to life? Our lost boy is restored to us after all of these years. Come into the light so I can take a good look at you."

He seized Miles roughly by the arm and pulled him toward the window. Then he examined Miles from head to foot with his eyes. He turned Miles from side to side, frowning and stepping briskly around him.

"Go ahead and examine me," Miles said. "I am your brother."

Miles was about to embrace his brother, but Hugh put a hand up to stop him. He said, "What a horrible disappointment!"

For a moment, Miles was amazed and could not speak. Then he asked, "What is a disappointment? Am I not your brother?"

"I'm afraid that I do not recognize you," Hugh said. "I received a letter six or seven years ago. It said that my brother died in battle."

"It was a lie!" Miles cried. "Call Father. He will know me."

"I cannot, for he is gone," Hugh said.

"Father is dead?" Miles asked. His lip trembled. "Half of my joy is gone now. Call Arthur, surely he will know me and console me."

"He is also dead," Hugh said.

"Gone!" Miles said. "Please tell me that the Lady Edith is alive and well. I could not bear to hear that she is gone as well."

"Yes, she lives," Hugh reported.

"Then I have some joy left," Miles said. "Bring her to me. Surely she will know me. Bring the old servants, too. They will recognize me."

Hugh told Miles that five servants only remained. When he named them, Miles thought it was strange that the five dishonest servants were still there, while all of the trusted ones were gone.

The king walked over to his friend. "Do not worry," he said. "There are others in the world who have had their true identity denied. You have company."

"Wait and see," Miles said. "I am not an impostor. Lady Edith will prove it. Please do not doubt me. I could not bear it."

"I do not doubt you," the king said. "Do you doubt me?"

Miles felt guilty. He had not believed the boy. Fortunately, Hugh came back

into the room and saved him from having to answer.

A beautiful lady followed Hugh. She walked slowly with her head bowed. She looked very sad.

Miles sprang forward. "Edith, my darling," he cried.

Hugh stopped him. He asked Lady Edith if she knew the man who stood before her.

Edith's cheeks flushed and she trembled. For several moments, she stood still. Then she lifted her head and looked into Miles' eyes. The blood drained from her face. "I do not know him," she said. Then she sobbed and ran out of the room.

Miles sank into a chair and covered his face with his hands.

Hugh asked the servants if they recognized Miles. They stared blankly and said they did not.

"My wife did not recognize you," Hugh said coldly.

"Your wife!" Miles shouted. Then he pinned Hugh against the wall, holding

him by his throat. "You scoundrel! You wrote that letter yourself. And you stole my beloved!"

Red-faced and almost suffocated, Hugh staggered to the nearest chair. He commanded the servants to seize and bind the stranger. They hesitated, because Miles was armed and they were not. Hugh ordered them to go and get their weapons. He warned Miles not to try to escape.

"Escape?" Miles said. "Miles Hendon is master of Hendon Hall. I will remain here. Do not doubt it!"

## CHAPTER 20
# Disowned

Miles thought that the Lady Edith had acted very strangely. He was sure that she had recognized him.

While Hugh and the servants were getting their weapons, Edith came back into the room.

Miles jumped forward to meet her, but she stopped him.

"Sir, I have come to warn you," Edith said sadly. "Do not stay here. It is dangerous." She hesitated, then said, "You look like what our lost lad would have grown to be, had he lived."

"I am Miles," he said. "Please say that you know me."

"I believe that you truly think you are," she said. "But my husband rules this region. He is wicked and cruel. There is no limit to his power. You are in grave danger here."

"He has commanded you to betray and disown your childhood friend," Miles said reproachfully. A tear came to Lady Edith's eye.

"Please leave," she said. "Hugh is a tyrant who knows no pity. Take this money and bribe the servants to let you pass. Escape while you can."

Just then, the servants burst into the room, and a violent struggle began. Miles was overpowered and dragged away. The king was taken also, and both were bound and led to a prison.

The prison cells were crowded. Miles and the king were chained in a large holding room with twenty prisoners. The king was outraged by this indignity, and Miles was bitterly disappointed. He knew that Lady Edith had recognized him.

During the next week, men whose faces Miles remembered came to see him. They all claimed not to know him. To make matters worse, they jeered at him and insulted him.

One day, the jailer brought in an old man. It was Blake Andrews, a kind, honest servant who had worked for Miles' father. Miles was sure that Andrews would recognize him.

The man glanced around. He claimed that he did not recognize anyone. He asked the jailer to point out the imposter. He swore that Miles was not who he claimed to be. The jailer laughed and walked out of the room.

As soon as the jailer was gone, Blake came close to Miles. "It's a miracle," Blake whispered. "You are alive, sir! Say the word and I will go forth and make your presence known!"

"Please don't. It would ruin you," Miles said. "But I thank you. You have restored my faith."

The old servant became very valuable to Miles and the king. He visited several times a day, bringing them food and the latest news.

Little by little, Miles found out the story of his family. Miles' brother Arthur had died six years earlier. Grief stricken by the loss of two sons, Miles' father became gravely ill. He wished to see Hugh and Lady Edith wed before he died. Edith did not want to marry Hugh and begged for a delay, hoping for Miles' return. But when the letter came telling of Miles' death, the wedding took place. Soon after, Miles' father died.

Andrews reported rumors that the king was mad.

"The king is not mad, old man," Edward said.

"The late king is to be buried at Windsor Castle in a day or two. The new king will be crowned at Westminster Abbey," Andrews continued.

"I think they need to find him first," the king muttered under his breath.

Andrews reported that Hugh was to attend the coronation.

"The coronation of whom?" Edward asked, alarmed.

"The king!" Andrews exclaimed. "We only have one, Edward the Sixth. All men praise him. He saved the Duke of Norfolk's life and is intent on abolishing the cruelest laws that oppress the people."

This news struck Edward dumb. He wondered if the king was the beggar-

boy. Surely, Edward thought, the pauper's manners and speech would give away his true identity. Edward's impatience to get to London grew.

While he was in the prison, the king befriended some of the prisoners. Many of them had been sentenced to death for trivial offenses. The king vowed to abolish these cruel laws once he was reinstated as the rightful king.

# CHAPTER 21

# The Sacrifice

Miles grew weary of being confined. He thought that he would welcome any sentence, as long as further imprisonment was not a part of it. But he was mistaken about that. He was sentenced to sit for two hours in the stocks for impersonating himself and assaulting his brother. He raged and threatened his captors as he was led to the stocks, but the officers roughly moved him along, paying no heed to his distress.

The king could not get through the crowd that swarmed behind Miles, so he had to follow in the rear, far away from his trusted friend. The king had almost been sentenced to the same fate as

Miles, but then was released with a lecture and warning.

When the crowd finally stopped, Edward found a spot from which he could see Miles. The mob jeered at Miles. Some people threw eggs at him.

The king was enraged that his friend was being treated so cruelly. He sprang across the open circle and confronted the officers. "Set him free at once!" the king cried. "I am the–"

"Do not mind him," Miles exclaimed in a panic. "He is mad."

Sir Hugh, who had ridden up the moment before, ordered the officers to give the boy six lashings with a whip. When the king was seized, he did not even struggle. He was paralyzed by the mere thought of the outrage he was about to suffer.

"Let the lad go, you heartless dogs," Miles yelled. "I will take his lashings instead."

"That is a good idea," Hugh said. "Let

the little beggar go. Give this man a dozen lashings in his place."

The king tried to protest, but Hugh promised that Miles would get six extra lashings for every word that the king uttered. While poor Miles underwent his punishment, the king turned away in horror. Tears streamed down his cheeks. He could not bear to see Miles suffering.

Miles bore the heavy blows with soldierly strength. This, and the fact that he saved the boy by taking his punish-

ment, quieted the crowd. Now they had a great respect for Miles.

The king ran up to Miles. "I cannot begin to thank you for what you have done for me," he said. "I, Edward, King of England, dub you Earl Miles Hendon!"

# CHAPTER 22
# To London

When Miles' time in the stocks was ended, he was released and ordered to never return to Hendon Hall. He didn't know where to go or what to do. Then he remembered what Andrews had told him about the new king. Maybe he could go to him and beg for justice, Miles thought. So he decided to go to London. His father's old friend, Sir Humphrey Marlow, might be able to help him prove his identity.

Miles looked at the king. He wasn't sure if the pauper would want to return to a city where he had known only suffering. He turned to the boy and said,

"Where are we bound, good sir? What are your commands?"

"To London," the boy answered.

Miles was relieved by this answer—but astounded by it, too.

They arrived at London Bridge the night before the new king's coronation. The festivities had already started, and huge crowds were celebrating. In the mass of people, Miles and the king were separated from each other once again.

\*\*\*

While the real king wandered about the land poorly clad, poorly fed, and mistreated, the mock king, Tom Canty, enjoyed a much different experience.

Tom liked his new life. He had become used to being waited upon. He even enjoyed sitting in the council. He enjoyed his splendid clothes and ordered more. He found that four hundred servants were too few for him.

During his first few weeks at the castle, Tom felt very guilty about the fate of the real prince. But as time moved on and the prince did not return, Tom's mind became occupied with his new experiences.

Tom tried to forget about his mother and sisters, too. At first, he longed to be reunited with them. Now, the thought of them one day showing up in dirty rags made him shudder. He was glad that he did not often think of them, because he felt terribly guilty whenever he did.

Near midnight one February evening,

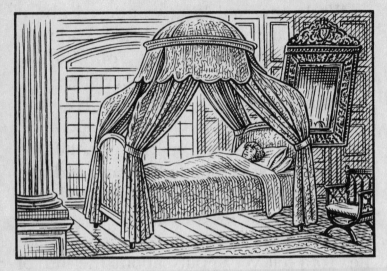

Tom sank into a peaceful sleep in his luxurious bed in the palace, guarded by his loyal servants. Tomorrow, he would be crowned King of England.

At the same time, Edward was wedged in among a crowd of people. He was hungry, thirsty, soiled, and worn with travel. The crowd was watching gangs of workmen, who streamed in and out of Westminster Abbey. They were making the last preparations for the royal coronation.

# CHAPTER 23

# The Recognition Procession

The next morning, Tom was the chief figure in a wonderful floating parade along the Thames River. According to ancient custom, the recognition procession that wound through London started at the Tower.

Dressed in splendid robes, Tom mounted a prancing war steed. The guards gathered in single file on either side of the king. They were followed by a regal procession of noblemen.

It was a brilliant spectacle. Cheers rose skyward as the procession moved through the multitudes of citizens.

Tom gazed over the sea of eager faces.

His heart swelled with pride. He felt that the one thing worth living for in this world was to be a king. Then he caught sight, at a distance, of a couple of his ragged Offal Court friends. His pride swelled more than ever. Oh, if they could only recognize him now! What unspeakable glory it would be! But he had to choke down his desire, for such recognition might cost him his new position. So he turned his head away.

The great parade moved on, passing under one triumphal arch after another. Colorful banners and streamers hung from every house and window. Tom was amazed that all of these wonders were planned in his honor. The mock king's cheeks flushed with excitement. His eyes flashed.

Just as he was raising his head, he caught sight of a pale face straining forward, its intense eyes riveted upon him. A sickening feeling struck through him. He recognized his mother! He put his

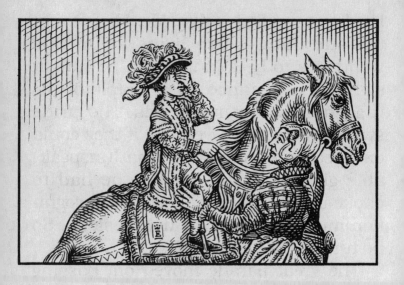

hand in front of his face.

His mother stormed past the guards and embraced Tom's leg. "My child!" she cried.

One of the king's guards snatched her away. Tom said, "I do not know you woman." As soon as he said it, he felt heartsick. She seemed so broken-hearted.

The procession moved on, but Tom's actions played over and over in his mind.

CHAPTER 24

# Coronation Day

As Tom was riding through the streets of London, Westminster Abbey was beginning to fill with nobles and their ladies arriving for the coronation, dressed in their finest attire. Some people had been waiting for more than five hours.

Finally, the triumphant sounds of music rang out. Clothed in a long robe of gold cloth, Tom appeared at the door and stepped onto the platform. The guests rose, and the ceremony began.

Then Tom was conducted to the throne. His face was ashen, his heart heavy and remorseful.

The final act was at hand. The Archbishop of Canterbury lifted up the crown of England from its cushion and held it over the boy's head.

A deep hush fell over the abbey. At this impressive moment, a startling vision intruded upon the scene—a vision which nobody in the abbey had seen when it first appeared. It was a poorly dressed boy. When he boldly marched up the central aisle, everyone turned their eyes on him.

He raised his hand regally. "I forbid you to place the crown on that imposter's head," Edward proclaimed. "I am the real king!"

In an instant, several hands grabbed the boy. But at the same time, Tom rushed forward. "Let him go," Tom ordered. "He *is* the king!"

Astonishment swept through the assembly. The guests partly rose in their places and stared at one another and at the two nearly identical boys.

The Lord Protector was shocked. "Do not mind him," he said. "His mind is disturbed. Seize the vagabond!"

Tom would allow no such thing. No one moved or spoke. No one knew how to act or what to say in so strange and surprising an emergency. Edward moved steadily forward and stepped up to the platform. He fell on his knees before the real king. "Oh my lord, put on thy crown!" he cried.

The Lord Protector decided to test Edward to determine whether he was who he claimed to be. He asked the boy many questions about the court, the late king, the prince and the princesses. The boy answered all of the questions correctly, without hesitating. He described the rooms of state in the palace, the late king's apartments, and those of the Prince of Wales.

The Lord Protector shook his head. He said that Tom could answer all of those questions, as well. There was still

no proof that Edward was the real king.

Then the Lord Protector had an idea. "Do you know the location of the Great Seal?" he asked Edward. The Great Seal had not been found since the day that Tom arrived at the palace. Only the real king could solve the mystery of the Great Seal's whereabouts.

"It is in the bottom left hand corner of my private closet," Edward said.

A messenger was sent to check the location. Everyone in the room waited in suspense. Finally the messenger returned.

"The seal is not there!" he reported.

"Cast the beggar into the street," the Lord Protector cried.

Again Tom ordered them to stop. Suddenly his eyes lit up. "Was the seal round and thick?" he asked. Edward nodded. "Now I know where this Great Seal lies! If you had described it to me, I would have given it to you weeks ago. My king, please think. It was the very

last thing you did that day before you left the palace."

Silence fell over the assembly. All eyes were fixed on the beggar, who stood thinking. Minutes passed while the boy struggled to remember. His lip trembled.

"Do not give up," Tom pleaded. Then Tom went over every detail of the events of that fateful morning.

Suddenly, Edward remembered! "The Great Seal hangs behind my suit of armor!" he cried.

All the assembly were on their feet now. They waited impatiently as the messenger was sent to check for the Great Seal.

When the messenger rushed back into the room, he held the Great Seal in his hand. Then a loud shout was heard throughout the room. "Long live the king!" Both Edward and Tom breathed sighs of relief.

For five minutes the air quaked with shouts and the crash of musical instruments. The sky was white with a storm of waving handkerchiefs. Through it all, a ragged lad, the most conspicuous figure in England, stood flushed and happy and proud in the center of the spacious platform.

"Now, my king, take these royal garments back and give poor Tom, your humble servant, his shreds and tatters," Tom requested.

The Lord Protector said, "Let the small imposter be stripped and flung

# *The Prince and the Pauper*

into the prison."

But Edward, king once again, would not hear of it. "If it were not for him, I would not have my crown back," he said.

The beautiful royal robe was removed from Tom's shoulders and put on Edward's. Then the coronation ceremony resumed. The real king was anointed

and the crown set upon his head. All of London seemed to shake with applause.

# CHAPTER 25

# Prince Edward Takes His Throne

As Tom and King Edward were exchanging identities for the second, and final, time, Miles Hendon was searching frantically for his companion. He wandered along every street in London, but there was no sign of the boy. He had vanished!

It occurred to him that his father's friend, Sir Humphrey Marlow, might be of some assistance. So Miles turned his steps toward the palace. Outside the palace gates, Miles stumbled into the whipping boy.

In his frenzy of concern for Edward, Miles was quite a sight. He was tired and

out of breath. He managed, in a choked voice, to say to the whipping boy, "Do you know Sir Humphrey Marlowe?"

The whipping boy was startled by the question. "Of course I do," he said. "Sir Humphrey Marlowe was my father. I'm sorry, sir, but he has died."

Miles was heartbroken when he heard this latest bit of bad news. The whipping boy looked closely at Miles, who was shaking and hanging his head in despair. "You look a lot like someone that the king has been talking about ever since he returned," the boy said. "I'll take you into the palace. You might find what you are looking for there."

When they entered the palace, Miles was greeted with an even greater shock. The young king sat under a canopy of state with his head bent to one side. When the king raised his head, Miles saw that the king was his little ragged companion.

"The Lord of the Kingdom of Dreams is actually on the throne," Miles whispered under his breath. "Could it be that the boy I took for a common pauper is really the King of England after all? There is one way to find out."

Miles confidently strode to the wall, picked up a chair, and placed it in front of the canopy. Then he sat down and looked up at the king. A hand reached out and grabbed Miles by the shoulder. "How dare you sit before the king!" a voice cried.

"Do not touch him," King Edward

cried out. "This is my trusted servant, Miles Hendon. He has saved me from harm and possible death on many occasions. For this, he is to have special consideration at this court. He is not only a knight by royal decree, he is a peer of England, Earl of Kent. He shall have gold and lands and live in safety and high esteem.

"The privilege that Sir Miles has just exercised has also been granted by royal decree. We have ordained that the earl and his heirs shall have and hold the

right to sit in the presence of the Majesty of England," King Edward declared triumphantly. Miles continued to gaze at the king with a dazed look on his face.

Just at that moment, who should enter the hall but Sir Hugh and Lady Edith! They were as amazed as Miles to see what was happening. They stood bewildered and looked from Miles to the king, and then back again.

Miles did not see them. He was staring at King Edward. He murmured, "This is my little pauper! I am ashamed for doubting his word." He dropped upon his knees and placed his hands between the king's hands, swearing allegiance in return for the gold, lands and titles that the king had bestowed on him.

The king had seen Hugh and Lady Edith. He said to his guards, "Strip this thief of his stolen estates and put him under lock and key, where he can no longer menace innocent people."

While the guards carried out their orders, there was a stir at the other end

of the room. Then the room became silent and the assembly parted for Tom, who marched down the aisle behind a royal usher. When he had gotten close to the canopy, Tom knelt before the king.

"I have heard the story of these past few weeks," King Edward said to Tom. "You have ruled well and governed wisely. By being fair and gentle with my subjects, you have earned my esteem. Therefore, your mother and sisters shall be cared for. Your father shall go to prison. You shall live on royal grounds in a home befitting a hero of the people."

Tom was moved by the king's words. He was sincerely grateful to the noble king, who had done so much for him and his family. He continued to bow, feeling ashamed of his own behavior toward his mother and former companions from Offal Court.

King Edward continued, "All of my subjects will treat you with respect and dignity. You will have the protection of the throne and the support of the crown."

Tom wasn't sure that he deserved the honors that the king had bestowed on him. In humility, he bowed his head. When he looked up, the king was looking straight at him. They had both been through so much during the past few days. Their lives had both been completely changed. Tom had gotten to see a side of life that he had only imagined, while Edward had seen a side of life that he had never imagined. King Edward's gaze remained steady. Tom returned his gaze, acknowledging their new bond.

"You shall now be called by the honorable title of King's Ward," King Edward pronounced. A cheer rang out from the assembly. Tom rose, determined to stand firm by King Edward throughout the monarch's reign.

# CHAPTER 26

# Justice for All

When all of the mysteries were cleared up, Hugh Hendon confessed that his wife had denied Miles' identity by his command. Hugh had threatened to harm her if she did otherwise. Lady Edith had stood her ground and told him to do what he pleased. She would not deny Miles. But when Hugh threatened to take Miles' life, she promised to do as Hugh wished.

Rather than be sent to prison for his evil doings, Hugh deserted his wife and escaped to France, where he died. Miles married his love, Lady Edith, and there were grand times and rejoicing at

Hendon Hall.

Miles and Tom were favorites of the king all through his reign, and his sincere mourners when he died.

Tom Canty lived to be a handsome, white-haired old fellow. As long as he lived, he was honored. He never forgot King Edward's kindness and noble actions. He defended his king through good times and bad. He still felt ashamed when he thought of how he had wanted to disown his family. From that time forward, he stood by them and helped in any way he could to make up for the years of hardship.

King Edward sought out all of the suffering people that he had met on his long journey back to the throne. He gave them comfortable homes and respectable jobs. He punished the official who had given Miles the cruel lashings upon his back, as well.

The people loved King Edward, who did everything he could to make up for all of his father's cruel laws. The reign of

Edward VI was a merciful one for those harsh times.

As long as the king lived, he was fond of telling the story of his adventures, from the hour that the sentinel cuffed

him away from the palace gate until he sat on the royal throne as the King of England.

**The End**

## About the Author

Samuel Langhorne Clemens was born in 1835 in Florida, Missouri. He spent most of his childhood in Hannibal, Missouri, a Mississippi River port city.

Clemens' formal education did not extend beyond grade school, but he received a broad education from his wide range of work experience, which included print shops and newspaper offices.

In 1853, he left Hannibal and spent the next decade working as a steamboat pilot, silver miner, soldier and newspaper reporter.

Under the name Mark Twain, Clemens wrote a number of classic novels featuring young heroes, including *The Adventures of Tom Sawyer* and *Adventures of Huckleberry Finn.* He took his pen name from a river phrase that means "two fathoms deep," or safe water for a steamboat.

Clemens is considered to be one of American literature's greatest humorists. He died in 1910 in Redding, Connecticut.